Willow's Worries

Written by
Katrina Humphreys

Illustrated by
Afton Jane

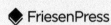 FriesenPress

One Printers Way
Altona, MB R0G 0B0
Canada

www.friesenpress.com

Copyright © 2024 by Katrina Humphreys
First Edition — 2024

All rights reserved.

Illustrator: Afton Jane

No part of this publication may be reproduced in any form, or by any means, electronic or mechanical, including photocopying, recording, or any information browsing, storage, or retrieval system, without permission in writing from FriesenPress.

ISBN
978-1-03-830031-7 (Hardcover)
978-1-03-830030-0 (Paperback)
978-1-03-830032-4 (eBook)

1. JUVENILE FICTION, SOCIAL ISSUES, EMOTIONS & FEELINGS

Distributed to the trade by The Ingram Book Company

For my daughters, who endlessly inspire me.
Thank you to my husband for always supporting me.

This is a story about Willow, who is seven years old. Willow likes her pet lizard Harry, drawing cats, exploring nature, and playing with her friends.

But Willow's favourite thing to do in the world is play **soccer**!

When she's not at soccer practice with her teammates, she loves to go to her neighbourhood field and practice her soccer skills.

As much as Willow loves soccer, something new is standing in the way of Willow getting to the soccer field.

You might think it's because she has to feed her pet **lizard**...
Or because she has too much **homework**...
Or because she can't find matching **socks**!

But it's not—it's because
of her worries.

Willow hasn't always had worries, and they aren't always with her. Her worries come and go depending on what Willow's doing or how she's feeling.

Willow's worries
started at the beach...

It was a sunny and beautiful day, Willow and her family were doing one of their favourite things—walking at the beach together.

They love to walk in the mornings because the beach is quiet, the tide is far out, and all of the tiny crabs and seashells are easy to spot.

Willow loves to flip over the big rocks on the beach and see how many little **crabs** scurry out from under. She loves to hold the crabs and let their small pinchers **tickle** her hands.

That morning there were other families at the beach, too. Some of those families had their dogs with them. Dogs love to sniff, dig, and run around on beaches.

Most of the dogs were running and playing with their own families.

From the far side of the beach, a **big dog** came excitedly running toward Willow. She wasn't scared at first—but as it got closer, the dog didn't slow down.

In that moment, Willow started to feel panicked.

Not knowing what to do, she **froze**.

She didn't know what the dog wanted.

Why was it coming toward her?!

The dog bumped into Willow and went right past her. Willow fell down to the sand.

The dog didn't mean to bump into Willow, it was only excited; but it scared Willow, and she started to cry. The dog ran back to their owner, unaware that it scared Willow.

Willow's mom helped her up.
"Are you okay, honey?" she asked.

Willow was startled and upset.
"Can we leave?" she asked.

A few days later, Willow asks her dad,
"Can we go to the soccer field?"

"Of course we can, sweetie," her dad says. Willow
couldn't be happier! She loves any chance to kick
her ball around.

Willow doesn't know that a new worry
is waiting for her.

When they get to the field, Willow sees
a lot of dogs running around and playing catch
with their owners.

She starts to feel nervous and scared that the dogs are close to her.

Willow begins to worry.

Watching the dogs on the field, Willow can feel her **heart beating** faster, and she feels a little **sweaty**. Willow's **stomach hurts** and her **body shakes**.

Willow realizes she can't concentrate
on playing soccer because her worries are
distracting her.

"Dad, can we go home?" she asks.

"Already?" he asked, surprised.
"We've hardly played at all."

"I know." Willow is sad, but she doesn't know how
to explain her worries to her dad. They go home,
and Willow puts her soccer ball away.

Since that day on the beach, Willow feels nervous when she sees dogs. Her worries can start before she even sees a dog, when she just wonders if dogs will be at the field at all.

Willow's worries don't always make her feel sweaty, or shaky, or make her heart beat fast. Sometimes she feels more than one of those things at once—other times none at all.

Willow's worries don't only get in the way of her playing soccer. They get in the way of her going for a walk in the forest, playing at a playground, or going to a friend's house that has a pet dog.

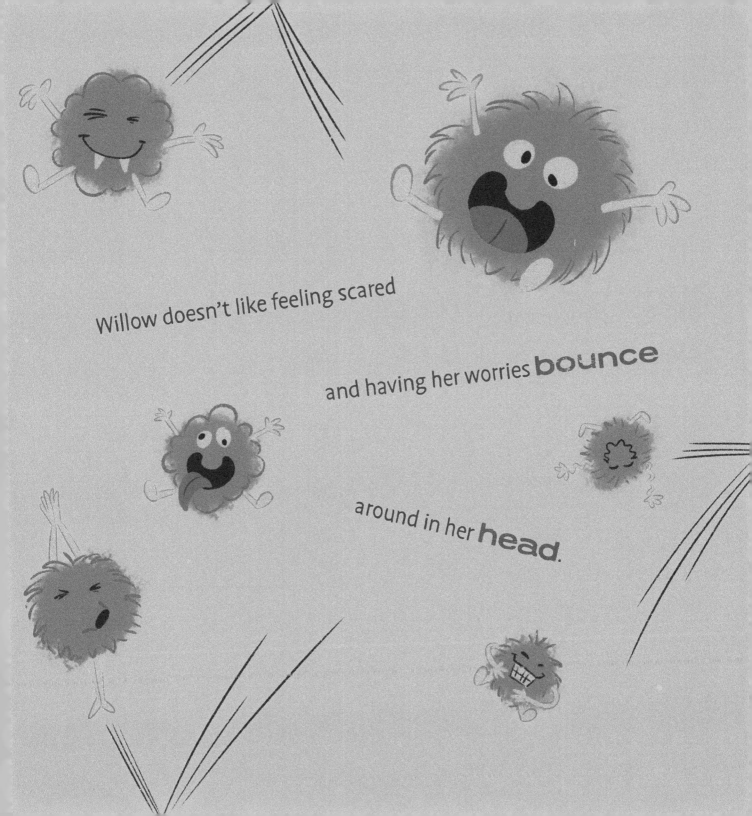

Willow doesn't like feeling scared

and having her worries **bounce**

around in her **head**.

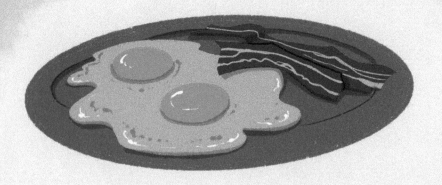

One day, Willow's friends ask her to play soccer with them at the field. She finishes her breakfast that morning feeling **strong**. She's going to stand up to her worries!

As Willow is getting ready for soccer, she can feel her worries cropping up in her head. The worries are telling her that there might be dogs at the field. These thoughts bring up more worries.

Willow takes a **breath** and says to herself, " I can do this." Saying these words helps her quiet the worries in her head.

But as she puts her shin pads on, those worries start to **grow**.

As she pulls her socks over her shins, the worries get **louder and louder**, reminding her that the dogs might be running free of their leashes.

Willow closes her eyes and takes another **deep breath**. She tries to settle her worries. "Dogs are kind, and usually stay close to their owners," she reminds herself. "And I'll have so much fun playing soccer!" This helps to make the worries quiet down.

As Willow laces up her cleats, she makes a deal with herself. "All I have to do is get out the door and go to the soccer field. I don't have to stay the whole time. If I feel too scared, I can leave."

This **goal** helps Willow feel confident that she can go to the field without feeling trapped into staying there. When it comes to **conquering** her worries, it's about taking little steps, one moment at a time.

Willow grabs her soccer ball and heads to the field filled with excitement!

As she walks to the field, Willow whispers to herself, "I can do this, I am strong." With every step she continues to remind herself how **strong** she is, and how much fun she has when she plays soccer.

When Willow gets to the field, she sees a dog playing catch with their owner. Her hands start to feel a little sweaty.

She takes a moment to stop and watch the dog from a comfortable distance.

What Willow notices is that the dog picks up the ball and runs right back to their owner to give them the ball. Then, the dog waits patiently at their owner's feet for the ball to be thrown again.

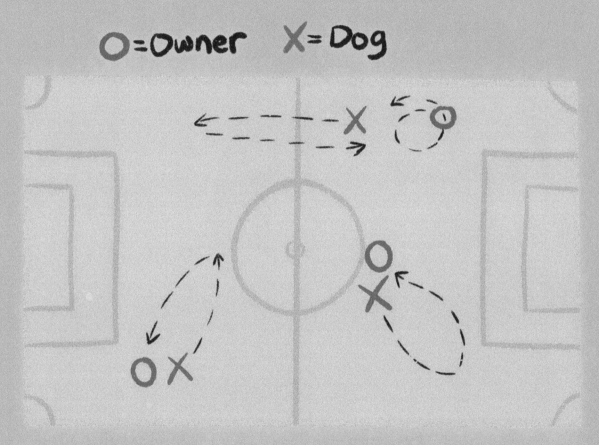

Watching the dog do this over and over helps Willow feel **calm**.

"*See?*" she thinks. "*The dog won't run at me, all it cares about is the ball!*"

Feeling better, Willow walks over to the soccer field.

When she gets to the field, all of her friends are there. They split up into two teams and start the game.

Before Willow knows it, she's having so much **fun** that she barely looks around for dogs. She scores a goal that day, and her team wins!

Willow is proud of her team for winning the game.
But what she feels the most proud
of is **herself**.

She didn't let her worries get so loud that she
missed out on something she loves.

About the Author

Katrina Humphreys has a Bachelor of Fine Arts, Photography, from Emily Carr University of Art + Design. She has worked with young children, teaching them art and photography at her local community centres. When someone close to Katrina dealt with anxiety, she helped them work through it. Katrina was inspired to write this book to help children with anxiety feel comforted and their parents feel supported in guiding their children through fear and anxiety. When not taking photographs and writing, Katrina loves running and spending time outdoors with her family, especially on a lake or at the ocean. She lives in beautiful Vancouver, Canada, with her husband and their two daughters.

Printed in the USA
CPSIA information can be obtained
at www.ICGtesting.com
LVHW072154040924
790133LV00056B/663